The Story of Nib: A Story about Finding Yourself

Published by Gatekeeper Press
2167 Stringtown Rd, Suite 109
Columbus, OH 43123-2989
www.GatekeeperPress.com

The cover design, interior formatting, typesetting, and editorial work for this book are entirely the product of the author. Gatekeeper Press did not participate in and is not responsible for any aspect of these elements.

ISBN (hardcover): 9781662914881

To my Love. Thank you for giving me back to myself.
A & K all the way.

To my kids, R, L, C, J, and E, I love you all so much.
Always be on the lookout.
You never know where you might find yourself.

I thirst for sun.
Darkness boxes me in.
Finally, streams of light through the corners.
The light rushes in.
I can't see. It's too bright. Sun and sky clear overhead.
Blurry figures stand at the edge.

    Friend or foe,

I will not know for a time.
All are considered foes presently.
Untrusting, I reach for an outstretched hand.

The tight grip is unlike anything I've felt.
The scent of safety and security wafts from the three figures before me.

One small,

one medium like me,

and one large.

They smile and talk at me.
I can't understand them, but their smiles seem sincere.
They've come though, for what?
To move me to new darkness?
To let me taste this open field, but lead me back to the shadows?

I can tell they want something from me.

                              Or want me to do something.

I decide that these who provided light after all these years deserve some trust.
I hold tight to the hand that holds mine and step out.

The feel of the grass against my dirty skin.

They talk but I still don't understand.

The breeze feels so good, gliding over me,
carrying away some of the stench that surrounds me.

I stand as still as a statue, unsure of what comes next,
but certain I don't want this moment to end.

The little one motions for me to sit beside her on the grass.
She has an innocence about her that I can't help but trust.
I oblige, still not able to understand her, but I understand she's safe.
She puts her hand up, showing all five fingers.
Instinctively I reach out, pressing the flesh of my palm against hers.
Her hand is so little, but her skin is so warm and smooth.
The comfort and strangeness of her touch surge through my whole body.
She doesn't care that my hands are dirty.

She seems excited by my mere presence.

She starts a game,
exchanging high fives in between clapping.
Her giggles make me smile.
Not a full smile, but what's there is real.
The energy from this little one is contagious.
She moves faster and faster, slapping hands with me,
all the while her unrestrained hair flailing wildly.
She erupts into full-course laughter as the game ends,
falling back contented on the grassy carpet.
I do the same, and stare up into the expanse above.
So blue, unlike anything I've seen,
dotted by little white ships.
The air is the freshest I've ever tasted.

The little one sits up, so I do the same.
The big one sits down and places a plate on the grass.
The fruit, cheese roll-ups, and peanut butter
and jelly sandwiches look inviting,

but is this a trap?
The little one dives in, hands first, and lets me know
they're safe to eat by taking a huge bite.

Until this moment, I didn't realize how hungry I was.

I eat.

This simple food, comforting me to my deepest bone,
filling my body and soul.
I eat until I feel I might burst.
Nobody constrains me.
This freedom feels unnatural, like a newborn foal trying to walk,

but it also feels right.

I finish and the little one stands up and grabs my hand.
She hurriedly pulls me to my feet, excited for me to follow her somewhere.
She holds my hand and half pulls, half drags me after her.
I have no choice except to follow, but I don't mind.

She makes me feel safe.

The other two follow, talking quietly between them,
words I still cannot understand, although I think they are talking about me.
We walk for what seems like an eternity, through this vast field,
coming to a house on the edge of the woods.
We stand, looking at this house, the little one presenting it to me
like a prized possession, both hands open to one side as if to say,

"ta-da!"

She is proud.

I am tentative.

The house is stark white against the lush green of the forest's edge.
There are gables and a porch that wraps around the front and out of sight.
The seven steps leading to the door are spacious and inviting.
The little one scurries up, and when she reaches the top,
she turns back, motioning for me to join her.
I deliberately climb the steps, taking them one at a time,
my mind wondering if I am headed back toward darkness,
my body knowing that I am moving toward safety.
I reach the top, and the other two follow, hemming me in from behind,
a feeling of security beginning to take root.
The little one pushes open the simple white door.

I inhale, stepping over the threshold.

The exhale that follows is like none that I've ever felt before.
Something about this place feels like home.
I follow the little one in and up the interior stairs.
At the top are many rooms. We go into the first one,
a small but spacious room with a twin bed, a small cedar chest,
and a picture window overlooking the field.
She motions for me to sit on the bed.
I just stand though, too afraid my filth will get the white bedspread too dirty.
Understanding my dilemma without me speaking any words,
the little one leads me out of the room, down to the end of the hallway,
and into the most restorative-looking space I've ever seen.

A claw foot bathtub sits opposite the door,

a window overlooking the woods directly above it.

The white tile on the floor looks like it is fresh out of the box.

The walls are white except the one the tub sits against,

which is the purest blue, reminding me of the sky

I had been looking up at minutes before.

The space makes me feel surrounded by warmth and love.

The older one steps up behind me and,

understanding that I don't understand her,

taps my shoulder and motions toward the full bath, bubbles piled high.

She points to the towels on the sink, and backs out of the room,

allowing me to close the door.

I move toward the bath, slowly removing
my torn, tattered, and dirty clothing.
In my nakedness I'm still covered in filth.
I gently lower myself into the bath,
layers of grime immediately peeling into the water.
I start vigorously scrubbing,
suddenly realizing how clean I can be if I work at it.
My hair is caked with mud.
No matter how hard I try, it won't come fully clean.
All at once my hair, down to my mid-back, becomes something horrifying.
It makes me feel like an imposter, like I'm playing pretend.
With a scream, in one fell swoop I reach for a pair of scissors
sitting on the ledge next to a small ficus, and start cutting.
I don't stop until I'm fully emptied, hair sufficiently short.

There, I'm no longer pretending.

The consequences of my actions hit me at once and I weep,
realizing I can also hear clearly.

I stare at the hair in my hands.

It represents all that I long to be, and everything that I'm not.

I release it into the water, which I now realize hasn't gotten any less clear.

I stand up though, completely clean.

I can hear voices whispering outside the door.

They're waiting to be with me.

To help me.

These are good people.

I wrap my new, fresh skin in a towel and step into the hallway.

I can tell immediately something is different.

In them. In me.

"Come with me, we can get you dressed,"

the big one says, and motions down the hall.

"Ok," I respond, eliciting her to freeze mid-stride.

Turning around, she smiles, tears streaming down her face.

"I'm Nia by the way," she says.

I nod and don't respond. I...don't know who I am.

She understands and turns and heads back down the hall, me happy to follow.

She turns left in the middle of the hall
into a spacious room with a big bed,
big enough for me to stretch all the way out on.

This space is safe.
These people are safe.

But I feel vulnerable in my nakedness, even inside of a towel.
Nia motions toward a double closet spanning the opposite wall.
"You can wear any of the clothes in there."
I walk across the room slowly, with my breath held.
I slide open the double doors, revealing an unimaginable wardrobe.
Dresses of every sort, button down and polo shirts,
t-shirts, shorts, skirts, shoes of every kind.
I finger a yellow chiffon sundress,
waiting so badly to drop the towel where I stand and put it on,
but I can't.
I won't.
Nia senses my dilemma and says again, "Pick anything you want."

"No, I can't," I respond.

"I have a secret."

"I can't wear whatever I want," I repeat. "I'm embarrassed."
Nia smiles. "There's no reason to be ashamed or embarrassed.
I have the same secret," she responds, it echoing in my head.

What?! How does she know my secret??

Still reeling from her response, the little one, whose name
I still don't know, pops around the corner and proudly announces,
"Me too! I have the secret too!"
At nearly the same time, the middle one buzzes past the doorway,
flatly saying as she goes, "Yeah...me too."
I can't believe what I'm hearing!
"We all have this in common dear, and it's not a secret.
You're safe here. You can be yourself."

Be yourself.

The thought is so overwhelming.
Who am I?   Who was I?   Who will I be?
Myself.
It feels good to hear. No expectations, just me.
Reading my mind Nia says, "There are no expectations of you here.
And that starts with what you wear."

Nia and the little one leave my room all at once,
as if knowing I need time to process.
Who am I is a heavy question.
Pondering it for just a moment,
without the expectations of others overwhelms me.
I reach for a t-shirt and lounge pants.
Deciding without deciding.
It's all I can do, without knowing more of myself.
I emerge from the room slowly as the little one races past.
"C'mon! It's dinner time!" I follow her down the stairs,
more certain with every step that I am safe here.
On the main level is a dining room
with an oak table with seating for 4.
I wonder what would happen if they rescue another stranger like me.
They'd have to get a bigger table. The table is piled with every good thing.
Inviting me to sit, Nia and I join the little one,
the other one wandering in slowly, taking her time.
As she pulls up a chair, Nia says, "Before we begin...,"
a phrase that puts me on high alert unsure of what comes next,
"girls, why don't you introduce yourselves."

"Hi, I'm Ant," the little one jumps right in,

"I know we've already met, or at least I feel like we have.

You have pretty hair, and I like your pants."

How does this little one, so innocent and sincere,

know how to make me feel so at home

and so insecure about myself at the same time?

"Ant, I like that name," I reply.

Nia's eyes turn to the middle one.

Turning from Ant to the one who is roughly the same age as myself,

I realize suddenly how much she and Ant look alike.

They have to be sisters.

It seems like her time works differently than everyone else's though,

and after a long pause she blurts out suddenly and flatly,

"I'm Tonya." Waiting for more and realizing there is none,

I say, "Nice to meet you."

With a mouthful she mumbles back, "Uh huh," already having dug in,

clearly indifferent to my presence.

"Ok, let's eat," says Nia.

The more I sit and become comfortable with these three humans,
the more I start to wonder who they are and how they found me.
They are certainly members of the same family,
as their resemblance is too much to be something else.

As we eat, Nia suddenly asks, as if she forgot to earlier,
"What is your name, and what pronouns do you use?"
A question I've never been asked in my life,
I'm unsure how to respond.
How do I answer such a question,
when I still have no idea who I am or who I was?
And does who I was impact who I am or who I am becoming?
Understanding that this question requires a short answer
but also a deep understanding of one's self, Nia says,
"It's ok if you don't have an answer right now."
Relieved I nod and go back to eating the best meal
I've ever had with this strange threesome.

After dinner, Nia invites me to sit on the big sofa in the living room with her.

I've been thinking about her question since she asked it.

As we sit, I say, "I feel like I know who I am a little bit,

or maybe who I want to become.

I also feel like I am understanding more about who I was.

How those things are the same and yet so different.

I want to tell you to call me one thing, but the pull of the other is strong.

Which is real? How do I know?"

Knowing I don't need an answer, Nia waits patiently, allowing me to continue;

"If I'm here, with you and your family who rescued me,

without any expectations like you said, then please use she/her pronouns for me."

Even saying this out loud makes me feel like more of an imposter

and imposition than I already am, but I trust them.

Wow, that feels good, both the decision and saying I trust.

After all I've been through, in the darkness for so long.

My mind turns to my past.

I don't remember who I am.

I don't know my name.

All I can remember is darkness.

I know that's not the whole of me, but I can't get beyond it.
Nia slides a notebook with the colors of the rainbow on its front,
and stretches out a hand, offering a pen.
"It can be helpful to write," she says.
Not an order; not an expectation, but an offer.
To help me uncover myself.
To help me unhide from my own Knowing.
"There's a spot out back that may be useful,"
she says as she stands and silently leaves me to my innermost thoughts.
Where to even begin?
The only place that I can even picture is the darkness,
so that is where I start.

I stand up, unsure of where "out back" even is.

As I move toward the kitchen, I see Ant across the room,

a mischievous smile on her face,

pointing through the kitchen to a back door.

She says nothing, but her outstretched arm shows the way.

I move through the kitchen toward an old wooden screen door.

It pushes aside easily, sighing contently as it opens

and slapping closed happily behind me.

Something inside me sparks.

The sound of the door, the sight of the woods behind the house,

the smell of the mid-summer heat rising,

all together resonating deeply, somewhere within.

Through the door is a porch, open to the woods but protected from the elements;

early evening sun streaming in through the forest canopy,

some of the beams making their way up and over the porch's wooden ledge.

This house, this space, these trees, the sun glinting off a far away stream

winding its way through the forest's dirt floor, all of it reminds me.

Hinting at another place and time where I knew who I was.

Where all things were possible.

I set pen and paper down on a side table next to a rocking chair.
I want to write but nothing comes.
I instead lean over the porch ledge and scream with all my might into the woods.
All of me releases into the summer air, cooled with a breeze that carries my pain,
my fear, my unknowing, my resonance, into the woods where the trees listen intently,
gently swaying and shaking their leaves in response.

I suddenly remember.

Night after night, day after day, screaming to be let out of the darkness.
My captivity, punctuated by silence in between my cries,
my screams for someone, anyone.
Screaming until I was hoarse; waiting for my voice to return
and screaming again until I collapsed.
Darkness and silence my loyal companions.
As my scream returns to me, much weaker after having been heard by the trees,
I look up to a hole in the roof.
The beam of light streaming through finds its way into my backbrain,
awakening new memories. It wasn't only darkness in my prison,

and I wasn't alone.

As I squeeze my eyes tight, the memories come back all at once.
Three beams of light stream into my dark prison through holes from above.
Each time I scream until exhaustion, I fall asleep,
awakening to food and water, tucked neatly in the corner.
Even with the light beams, I fumble to find the sustenance.
Knowing someone is out there makes me redouble my screaming efforts,
always ending in exhaustion, sleep, then more food and water,
more hope, and more screaming.

Day after day. I feel it in my body. The years piled up.

Twenty full years.

Each day etched deeply into the right wall of my confinement.
Years etched on the left. Twenty years of screaming.
Twenty years of loneliness. Twenty years of nobody.
Twenty years of sky seen only through a pinhole.
Twenty years lost. And for what?
Who did this to me? Who kept me alive?
And who was I before I became invisible?

The urge to write it down overtakes me.
I sit on the rocking chair with purpose,
grab the rainbow colored notebook and pen and start writing.
Something takes hold of me.
My time in darkness illuminated by my screaming,
the trees echoing back my story.
Confined on purpose. By someone.
Day after day, longing to see the sun, longing to stretch out,
my body growing bigger, taking up what little space there was to begin with.
My stench growing worse, month after month.

Nothing but my racing thoughts.
Nothing but my screams. Nothing but my lost voice.

Nothing.

I write about all the things I can remember.
Far away laughter, a few blades of grass finding their way to me.
Complete despair punctured by moments of hope.
Darkness, voices, screaming, sunbeams, exhaustion, grass.
Hope keeping me from leaving my body.
Hope that someday it would be different.
Hope that I would be found.

The creaking of the back door opening breaks my concentration and I look up
to see Nia standing there, a soft look on her face.
"I remember," I whisper.
"All of this, everything here is helping me to remember."
She smiles with a deep understanding and says,
"I just returned from where we found you. It helped me to understand you better,
I wonder if it could do the same for you."
I freeze, the thought of going back out there, voluntarily, makes my body shake.
Seeing the suggestion is a lot for me to handle, Nia says,
"If you ever decide to go, I can go with you if you'd like."
Tightness in my throat, I swallow and nod,
knowing what I have to do if I want to know who I am.
"I'd like that," I respond, more of a plea than a reply.
Not now though, I am exhausted.

Tomorrow.

I lie awake in my bed, content, a cacophony of noises hitting my ears.
Bullfrogs in a nearby pond, crickets chirping, bats squeaking, wind rustling leaves,
all remind me that I'm free.
Lying in the dark, legs stretched all the way out, I smile.
I don't know who I am, or why all this is happening,
but I know I'm not there. I'm here.

My eyes fly open. Darkness surrounds me. I'm back there.
I know what to do, I've been here before, I scream.

Suddenly, light invades my space. A doorway opens and a figure is standing there,
lit by a small night light in the hall. I am not there. I am here.
"Are you okay?"
asks Ant, standing no more than 3 and a half feet tall in an oversized nightshirt.
"I...I...,"
"It's ok," she says, throwing the door all the way open
as she scurries across the room and onto the foot of my bed.
"I'm with you now."

As we sit and talk, me and this little girl, so small and confident,

deep into the night, she asks, "Where did you come from?"

"I can't remember," I respond.

Reading my sadness she says, "I'm sorry, that must be hard."

She shimmies up the bed and throws her arms around me squeezing tight. "It's okay

though because you're here now. We can be sisters."

Sisters.

Tears appear in the corners of my eyes.

This little one, so young and yet so pure in her kindness.

"Don't you already have a sister?" I ask, mostly to satisfy my curiosity.

"Oh Tonya?" she responds, "Yeah, but she's soooo boring!"

Her eyes rolling from one side of her head all the way to the other.

"She's 13, goes on long walks without me and doesn't like to play

any of the games that someone my age likes to play."

"And what age might that be? I ask.

"I'm 6," she states confidently. "I mean I'm practically 6.

I'm 5 and 3 quarters, but I'll be six next month."

The moonlight reflects off of her cheeks as she smiles and asks, "How old are you?"

The innocence in her question unlocks something inside of me.
"I'm not really sure," I say. "Sometimes I feel like I'm 15,
but sometimes I feel like I'm 35.
Either way, I'd love to play games with you
and I'd be honored to be your new sister."
"Can I touch your hair?" Ant blurts out, pivoting our conversation abruptly.
"It just looks so soft and beautiful in the moonlight."
Her own hair, in a big braid careening over her shoulder
and into her lap is so much more beautiful than mine;
short, choppy, and undefined.
Again, the innocence and love I can feel coming off of
 her overwhelm my insecurities.
"Yes, you can," I say, giving her permission.
She slowly reaches up and her thumbs touch my forehead first
as she reaches for my hair with her other eight fingers.

Spark, flash, memories come flooding in.
Running, jumping, laughing, playing. Other kids. Hitting balls.
Climbing trees. Riding bikes. All at once I remember.
Not just glimpses but the whole of these memories are revealed.
The smell of a backyard barbeque,
the feel of chlorinated water from a neighbor's pool on my skin.
These are my memories, unlocked by the touch of this little one.
They provide my body with a much needed release
which comes in the form of sobbing.
Ant slowly removes her hands from my head, not saying a word,
but the smile in her eyes tells me that she knew this might happen.
She moves to be next to me, reaching her little arm up
to drape it across my shoulder while her other hand holds mine.
Exhausted, I close my eyes as the tears slow.
My Knowing is growing.

The smell of freshly baked bread and coffee awakens me,
nose first, as I open my eyes to get my bearings.
Was that a dream I had? I look over as the door opens a crack.
Ant, clearly waiting for me to wake up, peeks her head in.
"Breakfast is ready, and I'm sure you're hungry after last night,"
she says, confirming the reality of my new memories.
"That's the latest I've ever stayed up before!
It was 2 in the morning before I went to bed!"
I smile and open my arms.
Seeing what I need, she races towards me
and flies into my arms, hugging me tightly.
"Knowing is good right?" she whispers.
I nod and we release each other and move toward the door,
the stairs, and the kitchen.
I am excited for more, but anxious, unsure if I can handle it.

I follow Ant, who is dressed in the summeriest of dresses,

downstairs, past the table we ate at the night before and into the kitchen.

There is food of every color of the rainbow filling a small table in a breakfast nook.

Purple blackberries, red strawberries, orange cantaloupe, blueberries, cherries,

yellow peaches, eggs, bread, muffins, jams and juices.

I stop to take in the sight of it.

"We grow all our own fruit out back," says Nia, spying my awe out of the corner of her eye.

I push open the screen door.

Hearing its sigh brings all of the memories of last night rushing back.

I step out onto the same porch, letting the door slap shut behind me.

The sight before me is incredible.

The woods that I was screaming my sorrows into the previous night is an orchard.

Fruit trees of all kinds, co-mingling with the forest almost out of sight.

The urge to taste what's in front of me overwhelms me.
As I turn to go back inside, the sight of Tonya, brooding face,
in the middle of the orchard catches my eye.
Walking among the trees, none of the harvesting baskets
which are all stacked by the back door are in her hands.
Something seems to be on her mind.
She catches my eye and looks away quickly,
turning her back to me, ducking into the shadows.
Her image, her face, linger in my mind as I go back inside.
I fill an empty plate, piling it high with color, and join Nia on the front porch.
The porch, facing the rising sun, is warm and not yet too hot to enjoy.
As Nia and I sit in silence looking out over the lush grass
stretching out to the horizon I ask, "How did you find me?"
Pausing, Nia takes a deep breath and responds,
"You'll be ready to Know more only when your body tells you you're ready to return."

Return.

Again the word scares me.
I know now that these people won't return me to my darkness,
but I am still afraid to go back.
I nod and divert my thoughts, diving into the kaleidoscope of fruit in front of me.

Each morning is the same, Nia and I sit on the porch, she tells me about herself,
I strain to Know more about myself to no avail.
Each day she looks at me without asking a question,
holding something she can't yet give to me,
and each day I look at her and say, "Not today. Maybe tomorrow."
Days turn to weeks, weeks turn to months.
I play with Ant, I talk to Nia, I pick fruit. I learn what it's like to love.
I feel what it's like to be loved without condition.
But I'm still lost in my unknowing.
Until one morning I see Nia looking at me,
still holding something in and I say,
"Today."

Nia nods, as if expecting my answer, and looks at me and says,
"You lead the way." We set our empty plates on a table
just outside the front door and move toward the field.
I descend the steps, deliberately, taking each one at a time,
memories of my coming fresh in my mind.
The grass feels cool beneath my clean, bare feet as I step down off the last step.
I stand there, Nia standing strong beside me says, "It's been a year you know."
I take in this information. It's been a year.
The kindness of this family overwhelms me.
Nia and Ant, always making me feel at home,
helping me to get back to my own Knowing.
Tonya, always brooding, apparently typical behavior
for a 13-year old, but kind in her own way.
So much has changed, yet so much is the same.
I am no longer in darkness on the outside,
but my insides remain locked away, hidden from me, out of reach.
I've also worn the same clothes since the first day I arrived.
A t-shirt and comfy pants...for an entire year.

The significance of all of this is not lost on me as
I will my feet to move, heading out into the field.
The breeze glides over me as we walk, the sky so blue, reminding me that I'm alive.
We walk in silence for what seems like hours.
Just as I'm about to ask Nia if I'm heading us in the right direction, I see it.
We crest a hill and I freeze, the whole of my prison in full view.
I can't breathe, trauma overtakes my body at the sight of it.
Knowing surges into my body: I have to touch it. I continue forward, Nia by my side,
feet feeling like they are weighed down by concrete with each step.

We get about 50 feet from it and Nia stops.
I look at her, without words, pleading with her to come with me,
Knowing I have to do this alone.
Tears in her eyes, she squeezes my hand. I let go of her hand,
Knowing this is mine to do, but Knowing that she won't leave me ever again.

As I approach, the sight of it makes me hold down my own vomit,
my body feeling what it's like to be on the inside.
I get up next to it and stare. How was I ever inside this thing?
It couldn't be any more than 4 feet wide by 4 feet long
and no taller than 3 feet high.
Its lid, pin holes punched in it, leans against its side.
This close I can see its crude, rudimentary nature,
the wood cobbled together like a child carpenter's first project.
I'm terribly afraid that if I get too close, I'll fall in,
lid closing over top of me forevermore.

I can't breathe.

My head starts to spin and I reach out to brace myself,
my hand touching a rough edge.

Spark, flash, memories. I remember following someone here.
A discussion. Someone tells me to look inside.
I do.
I fall headfirst.
In an instant, the lid closes behind me and darkness closes in around me.
I try to push up and out but nails are already being pounded in
and I am so weak, so innocent.

I inhale deeply, regaining my center of gravity,
opening my eyes to realize I'm still standing, Nia watching in the distance.
My memory flashes from present to past,
I can't make out who it was that locked me up.
I try, but the memory is too blurry.
I inhale long and deep, slowly exhaling it all out,
Knowing this thing has no power over me anymore.
Knowing there is more to know, I turn and walk back to where Nia is standing.
She shakes her head, anticipating my next question before I ask it.
"Follow me," she says quietly.

We walk in silence all the way back to the house.

My anticipation is palpable while so is her trepidation.

We arrive at the front steps, just like one year ago and enter the front door.

Nia motions me over to the couch and we sit.

We sit in silence, seconds dragging on, until I realize I am holding my breath.

As soon as I exhale, Nia starts talking.

"Last year, the day that we found you,

after we ate and you went out to the back porch to write,

I told you I visited the site where we just were. I too needed answers.

I walked there alone. I wept for you. I touched it, and when I did,

I felt as though I was responsible for putting you in there.

This thing is on my land after all, and I didn't even know about it.

I never came for you. But the more I sat with it,

I realized I couldn't have known, something had kept me from Knowing.

Then it became clear."

"The morning that we found you, Tonya suggested we go for a walk after breakfast.
It wasn't unusual for her to go for walks, as you know.
She goes for walks quite often and has for some time.
What was unusual was that she suggested we go with her.
Of course Ant and I were happy to join her,
if only because we both thought it a rare treat to be with Tonya.
We packed a lunch of fruit, cheese roll-ups and peanut butter and jelly sandwiches,
her favorites, and set out on our journey.
She led the way since it was her idea,
but it wasn't until we had been walking for a while
that I realized she was leading us out towards her special place.
I say it was her special place because many times when she would go out for a walk
she would say, 'Let me be. I'm going alone to my spot,' and she would head out
in the same direction. We never followed her, knowing she wanted to be alone."

"Now though, she was leading us to her special place, her spot.

Her own private walking grounds.

We had a lovely hike and as we were crossing over the last hill,

furthest from the house, we saw it. We saw you.

I sprinted ahead, yelling at the girls to stay behind me.

I ran so hard I almost slammed right into it.

I came so close I could hear you breathing inside.

I tried to rip the top off as fast as I could,

uncaring about what danger may be inside, Knowing it would be ok.

I motioned for the girls to help and together we all pried the top of it off

with all of our might, exposing you to the sunlight.

After a few moments, Knowing we had found something special, someone special,

I reached out my hand and you know the rest.

What I'm trying to say is, if it weren't for Tonya,

we never would have found you."

Tonya, this brooding teen who had hardly said more than a handful of sentences to me
in the last year, found me. I am shocked. I don't know what to say.
"I need to find her," I say suddenly, "I need to thank her."
I stand just in time to hear the sigh of the back door and to see a flash
of Tonya's back as she heads out the back door, it slapping loudly behind her.
I run to catch her but when I get to the back porch, she's gone, nowhere in sight.
Content to wait for her to return, I sit on the rocking chair,
Knowing now who I can thank for my freedom.
Why hasn't she ever told me this? It doesn't matter.
It's another piece of my story clicking into place and now I know
and I will show her how much I am grateful.
I sit on the porch for hours, waiting for her to return.
Nia joins me as the sun is going down.
"Why don't you eat something," she says.
"No," I say, "I want to be here when she returns."
But she doesn't return. I fall asleep on the porch,
the birds acting as my alarm clock the next morning. Tonya didn't come home.

I jump to my feet, panicked, worrying what terrible thing
has happened to her, and why she didn't come home.
I race through the house to find Nia.
When I don't see her anywhere on the main level, I check the front porch.
I find her sitting, staring out over the field.
"We have to search for her. We have to find her and make sure she's ok!" I shout.
Nia, remaining calm says, "She'll be ok."
Her calm reduces my anxiety, however I'm uncertain how she can be so sure.
Nia stands to go and make breakfast. "Please don't worry," she says.
"It will be ok. She always comes back. Let's get ready to welcome her when she comes home."
And with that Nia disappears into the house. Ok. She'll come back.

I can wait a little longer to thank the one who rescued me.

A day passes.

Then another.

Each day I rush down to find Nia, to see if Tonya has returned.
Each day Nia says, "Don't worry, she'll come back." At night I can't sleep.
I think of her out there, all alone. I wonder if she's ok.
With Nia and Ant asleep, I decide I have to find her.
I head out the back door into the orchard.
The moon is bright, illuminating spaces between the trees.
I search, gently calling her name.
After a while it hits me. Her special place!
I race back through the orchard past the house and into the field,
legs pumping as fast as they can.
The moonlight on the open space is a beautiful sight.
I want to stop and take it in, but I push the thought away as I run.
My sides burn, my shins hurt, on the verge of collapse,
scanning the field as I run. I crest the hill and see it.

In the moonlight it looks beautiful. All alone in the field.
My former prison. I slow down, if only to catch my breath,
stopping for a moment to put my hands on my knees.
As I stand back up I realize something is off.
I can see something inside of it.
I redouble my efforts, sprinting through the field,
reaching the box, memories attacking me from all sides.

There she is.

She doesn't look up.
I blurt, "I'm so glad I found you! Are you ok?
I needed to tell you how grateful I am for you finding me. Why did you run away?
Oh, I'm so glad you're alive!"
Tonya still doesn't look up. Is she ok? Can she hear me?
I dispense with wondering and grab her arm and stand her to her feet.
I hug her close saying "I don't know why you're out here,
but I'm so glad I found like you found me.
I love you so much and am so grateful to you."
Continuing to look down, tears streaming from her face she whispers,
"You don't understand, do you."

A statement more than a question. "I...I don't understand what?"
I fumble, taken aback by her crying and her statement.
"You still don't remember. You still don't Know!" she shouts through her tears.
"I know you scared me, I know your family took me in
after you found me, what don't I know?"
Her tears slow to a trickle as she looks down and whispers, "Everything."
She reaches out, still standing inside of it
and touches her thumbs to my forehead, fingers outstretched.

Spark, flash, memories. Walking out here with her long ago.
She asks me to get in. I'm confused.
Why would I get into this thing voluntarily; put myself into darkness?
She explains. It's for my own protection. I don't understand.
She says she is losing parts of herself.
She's been fighting, but has already lost a part of herself.
I am the most pure part of her that she has left. Pure Being.
She's afraid if I don't hide, she'll lose me too.
I cry. She cries. We hug. I turn.

I dive in, head first. Getting it over quickly like jumping into a cold pool.
She pulls the lid over me.

I have second thoughts.

I panic.

I try to push up but nails are already being pounded in and I am so pure, so innocent.
She promises to take care of me for as long as she needs to.
Until it's safe for me to come out. She'll protect me.
She won't lose any more of herself.
Day after day she comes, bringing me food and water.
Each day I ask if she can let me out. She says not yet. It's not safe.
She leaves and I scream until I have nothing left,
awakening to food and water, and her heavy breathing on the outside.
She tells me the world is a dangerous place. No place for me right now.
If she lets me out, she's not strong enough to protect me.
Then one day suddenly, she's gone. She doesn't return.
Food and water still come. But no company.
All alone.

I open my eyes looking into hers. These memories.

My memories, her memories, our memories.

"I am a part of you." I whisper my realization.

She slowly releases my head and says, "You are me. When we were young,

we were whole. Pure Being. Then the world changed us.

They took part of us when we were almost 6. Just gone.

We couldn't stand to lose anymore, so when they tried to take more of us, I fought.

I fought so hard. But I couldn't hold them off. I decided I would hide us.

Hide you, so I could go out and I wouldn't have to fight anymore.

There'd be nothing left for them to take. We hid you here.

I came every day until...I was too ashamed to come back.

Hiding you away changed me. It changed everything about me.

I lived a life they told me to live. Dead inside. I couldn't bear to see you.

I changed my name, my hair, my clothes, even my voice.

I got so good at pretending, I couldn't bear the thought of you

seeing me, hearing me that way.

I asked a friend to deliver food and water each night.

I'm so, so sorry, I just couldn't.

But then Nia found me."

As she says Nia's name, I hear a rustling behind me.

I turn just in time to see Nia and Ant coming to a stop a few feet behind us.

"Nia saved me," Tonya whispers.

"Me too," says Ant, gratefulness in her voice.

"And the only reason I was able to find them, find the strength

to find them, was because of you," Nia says, giving me a heartfelt look.

"I knew I was missing the purest part of me."

"Wait,...we're all...,"

"parts of a whole," Nia finishes my sentence.

"And I only went looking because you were hidden.

You stayed strong enough by hiding to help me keep going.

To help me find Ant. To help me find Tonya. To help us find you.

To help us find...ourselves."

As she finishes, the first light of dawn streams across the field,

letting me know I've been up all night.

I don't care. I am home. I am me.

I am who I always knew I was.

I help Tonya out of the box. Nia and Ant surround us with an embrace.

I know who I am. It's a surreal feeling.

Suddenly Ant shouts, "Now we can go to the city!"

I follow Ant's arm, pointing over the hill.

I see something, just illuminated by the early sun,

almost already retreating into the shadows. It is a city.

So far in the distance, I'm not sure it's even real.

How did I not notice it before?

The unknown creeps under my skin, making me afraid.

Afraid to be alone again. Afraid they'll leave me.

"Yes little one," Nia says gently, "We can go to the city, but only when she's ready.

We will always go where she goes now. And she will lead the way."

My fear, my loneliness, my shame, fades. My Knowing rises up.

"I think I'd like that Ant, but not just yet."

As we walk home, we talk about everything.
How Nia set out, feeling the pull of longing and emptiness, and found Ant.
The two of them living together, planting a garden,
realizing they were a vital part of each others' survival.
How Ant and Nia found Tonya one day walking,
alone and brooding, something on her mind.
Tonya tells me how she has lived multiple lives.
Pretending to be something, but being found
and returned to herself by Nia and Ant.
The three of them living together, content, but Knowing something was missing.
We talk about how memories, the memories
that Ant and Tonya gave me, are their memories too.
How they draw strength from me and I from them.
We arrive at home and together prepare breakfast,
none of us seemingly tired from the long night.
After breakfast I head to the porch where Nia already is sitting.
I pull out my brightly colored notebook.
I have to write after all of this. I have to write what I Know.
I glance over as I begin and see Nia, pulling out the same colored notebook.

Everything

I stop, a feeling coming over me.

Nia pulls out the notebook and pen and waves me over, patting the seat next to her.

I stand and move, sitting close to her.

She turns and looks at me, asking without asking. I nod yes.

She reaches her hands out, touching her thumbs to my forehead,

fingers reaching for my head. Spark, flash, memories. Her memories. My memories.

Memories somehow in the future and the past, written in her notebook, in my notebook.

Memories of finding myself, of family lost, and of friends gained.

I'm overcome with emotion and I weep.

Nia weeps, pulling her hands slowly away from my head.

"Thank you," I mouth still sobbing.

"Thank you," she whispers through tears, holding her hand over her heart.

We embrace, becoming one.

Every day after, Ant brings up the city. "Can we go today?"
And every day I shake my head saying, "No, I'm not ready yet. Maybe tomorrow."
Then one morning, Ant asks her question and I respond, "Today."
I realize I am still wearing pajama pants and a t-shirt, after all this time.
My mind floats to the yellow chiffon sundress in my closet.
"I think I need to go change first," I say with a smile.
"Then it's settled," Nia says. "I've packed a basket of food
and we will go with you. Ant, Tonya and me. You will lead the way."

I am overcome with feeling.

"By the way," Nia adds, "What is your name?"
I realize in that moment, that ever since I evaded her question
the first night I was home, she never asked again.
I pause, now Knowing the answer to her question..."I'm Antonia."
"Well Antonia," Nia says, "You better go get changed.
Oh and we have one quick stop to make on the way."
She holds the picnic basket of food
and opens the lid slightly, revealing a crowbar on top.

We all laugh and embrace as we get ready to go out on a new adventure, together.
Knowing that none of us will be in darkness alone ever again.

~~the end.~~

the beginning.

Thank you to everyone who helped birth this book into the world. This truly belongs to all of you. Thank you to all of our Kickstarter supporters who so passionately donated and shared this project with friends. Special thanks to Kickstarter supporters Fr. David Polich, Jennifer Yount, Tyler Higgs, Michelle Lippert Hukvari, Melissa Heidesch, Adam and Bri Brewster, Chris, Sarah, Izzie, and Gianna Chiaramonte, Emily and Mike House, and Drew Olivia Connelly, for your extra generous support.

Thank you Emily, Keri and Anna for helping me navigate and understand Kickstarter. This train would have never left the station without all of you making it happen. Thank you Kristin and Timothy for listening to me after my therapy sessions and helping me process what I was learning about myself, bringing these characters into focus.

Para Lluvia Velandia. Nunca imagine que conocería a alguién a un mundo de distancia, quien daría vida a mis palabras. Éste libro no sería nada sin tu arte increíble. Tu capturaste los sentimientos que estaban dentro de mi, y los dibujaste para que el mundo entero los pudiera ver. Estoy por siempre agradecida.

And to my love Katie, I truly don't know what to say other than you're my favorite.